M Adams

Memoir of Surgeon-Major Sir W. O'Shaughnessy Brooke

M Adams

Memoir of Surgeon-Major Sir W. O'Shaughnessy Brooke

ISBN/EAN: 9783337060954

Printed in Europe, USA, Canada, Australia, Japan

Cover: Foto ©Raphael Reischuk / pixelio.de

More available books at **www.hansebooks.com**

MEMOIR

OF

SURGEON-MAJOR

Sɪʀ W. O'SHAUGHNESSY BROOKE, Kт.,

M.D., F.R.S., F.R.C.S., F.S.A.,

IN CONNECTION WITH THE EARLY HISTORY OF THE TELEGRAPH IN INDIA.

COMPILED BY PERMISSION OF THE DIRECTOR-GENERAL OF TELEGRAPHS,

BY

M. ADAMS,

MEMBER OF THE HON'BLE SOCIETY OF THE MIDDLE TEMPLE, BARRISTER-AT-LAW, INDIAN TELEGRAPH DEPARTMENT.

———————

SIMLA:
PRINTED AT THE GOVERNMENT CENTRAL PRINTING OFFICE.
1889.

PREFACE.

A N application for a brief Memoir of the late Sir W.
O'Shaughnessy Brooke for publication in the journal of
a Scientific Society led to the search of the records in the
Office of the Director-General of Telegraphs, of the Calcutta Mint, of the Surgeon-General's Office, and the Proceedings of the Asiatic Society for the necessary materials.

The information thus gathered appeared to the Director-
General of Telegraphs as likely to be of such general
interest, that he has authorised its publication.

For much of the labour involved in collecting this information, I am indebted to Mr. W. Rees Philipps of the
Telegraph Department.

M. A.

SIMLA, *20th July 1889.*

MEMOIR

OF

Sir WILLIAM O'SHAUGHNESSY BROOKE, Kt.

Sir William O'Shaughnessy Brooke was born at Limerick in the year 1809. He entered the Bengal Medical Establishment of the Hon'ble East India Company's service on the 8th August 1833, and arrived at Fort William to take up his duties as Assistant Surgeon on the 10th December 1833. During the year 1834 he officiated in medical charge of the Civil Stations of Gyah and Cuttack successively, and towards the end of the year was doing duty with the artillery at Dum Dum, and later on was in medical charge of a detachment of the 72nd Bengal Native Infantry. In 1835, he was doing duty with the 10th Regiment Bengal Light Cavalry, and officiated as first assistant to the Opium Agent in Behar till the 5th August 1835, when he was appointed Professor in the Medical College at Calcutta. From the 26th October 1837 he was Secretary to the Committee on Materia Medica till the 23rd April 1840, when he was appointed Chemical Examiner to Government.

He acted as Lecturer to the Medical College at Calcutta, from the 15th May 1841, until the 29th November 1841, when he went on furlough to England on medical certificate.

On his return from leave, on the 24th January 1844, he was reappointed Chemical Examiner to Government. He officiated as Deputy Assay Master of the Calcutta Mint from the 7th November 1844 until the 14th January 1851,

when he was appointed to officiate as Assay Master of the
Calcutta Mint, having meanwhile, on the 5th December
1848, been promoted to the rank of Surgeon.

In 1852, he was appointed Superintendent of the Electric
Telegraphs in India. He was created a Knight Bachelor in
1856 for his services in connection with the establishment
and extension of the telegraph in India and promoted to the
rank of Surgeon-Major, on the 1st October 1858. On the
13th June 1860, he went on leave on medical certificate for
18 months, and finally retired from the service in 1862.
His death took place at Southsea on the 8th January 1889
after a short illness.

Sir William O'Shaughnessy assumed the name of Brooke
by Royal License in 1861. In addition to being a member
of several Medical Colleges and Societies, he was a Fellow
of the Royal Society and of the Society of Antiquarians.

He was the author of the following works and papers:

Bengal Dispensatory—Calcutta, 1842.
Explosion of Gunpowder under water by ⎫ Bl. As. Trans. 1839,
   Galvanic Battery   .   .   .   . ⎭   iii., p. 851.
Preparation of Ganja, &c.   .   .   . *ibid*, pp. 732, 838.
Communication of Telegraphic Signals,
   &c. . . . . . . *ibid*, p. 714.
Effects of Sea Water on Iron . . . *ibid*, 1843, xii., part 2.
Report on the Establishment of the Electric Telegraph (Pamphlet)
   published, Calcutta, 1852, by Government.
Bengal Pharmacopœia.

Most of Sir William O'Shaughnessy's contributions to general science are to be found in the journals of the Asiatic
Society.

His efforts in telegraphy are described in his Annual Reports of the Telegraph Department. He appears to have
taken a great interest in this subject from a very early
date, for in Article VI of the Journal No. 93 of the Asiatic

Society of Bengal, dated September 1839, are found his Memoranda relative to experiments on the communication of telegraphic signals by induced electricity. This paper was written when he was Professor of Chemistry at the Medical College, Calcutta, and contains a historical notice of the early telegraphs of Ronald and others, and also gives a detailed account of the experimental telegraphs erected by him in the Botanical Gardens, near Calcutta, in May 1839.

His own experiments on a line of iron wire 22 miles in length appeared to him conclusive as to the possibility of establishing a cheap electric telegraph. He also accidentally discovered that only "one insulated wire was requisite for completing communications" when the circuit could be completed by means of the earth, and he was surprised that Wheatstone should have patented a "five wired telegraph."

In his "Notes of Lectures on Natural Philosophy"* (the preface to which is dated the 16th January 1841), in the lecture on Galvanic Electricity, he speaks of having devised in 1839 a form of constant cell by using tanned sheep skin or paste-board, instead of pieces of bladder, which were at that time used where porous cells are now used. With ten of his cells he successfully blew up a sunken wreck at Fultah Reach on the 14th December 1839. To insulate the wire, on this occasion, he ran it through corks secured by pitch.

In his seventh lecture on "the Galvanic Telegraph," he describes the experiments he made in May 1839, with different instruments;† but he does not appear to have

---

* Extracts from Lectures VII & VIII will be found in the Appendix.

† Special attention is directed to the curious idea described in Lecture VII (see Appendix, page 26) of an A B C instrument, consisting of a lettered clock dial, combined with an induced current through the arms of the operator.

known in 1841, that a return wire was unnecessary to
complete a circuit, except in the case of a river intervening between the terminals. He, however, observed that
the return wire need not be insulated. About this time also
he conceived the idea of insulating underground wire by
burying a copper conductor in a trench rammed with pounded brick and mortar. He also proposed the use of the iron
rails of a railway as an insulated conductor.

The following extracts from the prefatory notice ap-
pended to a work by Sir W. O'Shaughnessy entitled *The
Electric Telegraph in British India—a Manual of in-
structions for subordinate officers, artificers and signallers
employed in the Department,* and published in London in
1853, will be read with interest as giving in his own words
the early history of the establishment of the telegraph in
India under the auspices of the author :

"In April and May 1839, the first *long* line of telegraph ever constructed in any country was erected by the writer of these pages in the
vicinity of Calcutta. The line was twenty-one miles in length, em-
bracing 7,000 feet of river circuit. The experiments performed on
this line removed all reasonable doubts regarding the practicability of
working electric telegraphs through enormous distances—a question
then, and for three years later, disputed by high authorities, and
regarded generally with contemptuous scepticism."

    *   *   *   *   *   *

"In 1850, a despatch from the Court of Directors to the Government of India re-called attention to the subject. The Government
addressed the Military Board of Bengal, and reports were called for
by the Board from Lieutenant-Colonel Forbes, of the Engineers, and
from myself.

"On these reports, dated December 1850, being placed before Government, an experimental line of telegraph, half subterranean, half
over ground, thirty miles in length, was directed to be constructed.

"This line* was commenced in October 1851, and opened to Diamond Harbour in December of that year. In the following May a

* On this line he used ⅜ inch iron rods, but on subsequent ones, rods of a smaller
gauge, ₁₆ inch, were employed as conductors.

branch was led to Moyapore. In August and December it was extended to Kedgeree, eighty miles distant by the line followed ; and in March 1852, the rivers Hooghly and Huldee were crossed, and the line from Calcutta to the sea opened for official and public correspondence.

"These results, having been duly reported, were under the consideration of the Supreme Government of India, when hostilities commenced in Burma. The services of the telegraph were thus brought into instant and practical requisition, and its incomparable capabilities tested with complete success. The *Rattler*, steam-frigate, bringing intelligence of the first operations of the war, had not passed the flagstaff of Kedgeree, on the 19th of April, when the news of the storming and capture of Rangoon was placed in the hands of the Governor-General in Calcutta, and posted on the gates of the Telegraph Office for the information of the public.

" On 14th of April 1852, Lord Dalhousie, as Governor of Bengal laid before the Government of India a long and deeply-interesting minute, in which his Lordship proposed the construction of lines from Calcutta to Agra, to Bombay, to Peshawar, and Madras; and the deputation of the author of this Manual to England, to give evidence before the Court of Directors, and assist in the dispatch to India of the requisite materials and stores.

" I left India on the 3rd of May 1852, and reported my arrival at the India House on the 20th of June. On the same day I had the gratification to hear from the Chairman of the Court of Directors, Sir James Weir Hogg, that the Governor-General's propositions, which arrived *via* Marseilles on the 14th, had been already sanctioned by the Court of Directors, and approved of by the Board of Control, and that a despatch from the Court was already on its way to India, in reply to the Governor-General's letter.

" Such rapidity in the dispatch of an important measure is, perhaps, without a parallel in any department of Government. All subsequent steps were taken with proportionate speed. The requisite contracts were issued for all the stores, before the 1st of August. Sixty enlisted artificers were placed in training at Warley; an inspection of the home and foreign telegraph lines undertaken, and completed by the 15th of November ; collections made of all the instruments in use in Europe and America : these pages prepared for the guidance of the persons to be employed on the works in India ;

and voluminous reports, with estimates and drawings, submitted from time to time on every step of these proceedings.

*   *   *   *   *   *   *

"The artificers are now on their voyage to the east, and in October next twenty camps of construction will be engaged in extending the web of telegraphs all over India."

In the same work Sir William O'Shaughnessy describes his experiences with underground and submarine lines. On page 72 he says—

"After many failures in attempting to coat the gutta-percha covered wire with lead, Mr. Chatterton has patented a process by which the coating of lead is applied on the gutta-percha cold   *   *   *   One hundred and twenty-eight miles of wire thus protected has been ordered   *   *   * chiefly for use in the great cities on the lines such as Calcutta, Agra, Delhi, Bombay, and Madras, in which the wire will be buried at a depth of three feet   *   *   *."

Some of this was dug up in Bombay in 1882, after a lapse of twenty-nine years in very good condition.

On page 75 he describes an underground line twelve miles in length from Calcutta to Bishtopore, which is chiefly remarkable from the fact of its being composed entirely of locally made material. It consisted of an iron rod for a conductor, ⅜ inch in diameter, covered with cloth, pitch and tar, and laid in roofing tiles half filled up with sand and resin. Remains of this line were dug up in 1888.

He had at first great difficulty in devising a suitable instrument for receiving signals owing to the strong natural currents peculiar to India, and after many trials he decided on a single needle horizontal galvanometer, which he found to be simple, cheap and efficient. But so difficult was it to procure material to make up even these simple instruments, that he had to enlist the services of two of his daughters for insulating, with silk fibre, the copper wire he required for the coils.

Sir William O'Shaughnessy's experiments in submarine work are interesting.

As early as 1849 his attention was drawn to this branch of telegraphy. He first tried a naked massive rod across the river, below the water, with repeating instruments on each bank, but without success ; for, to use his own words—

"It was found that the repeating instruments required to be attended by skilful and careful assistants, and that in practice such derangement occurred as caused very frequent interruptions."

He next tried to work across a river without any metallic conductor, "using the water alone as the sole vehicle of the electric impulses ;" and although he succeeded in transmitting signals, he found the battery power required for the purpose too enormous, and consequently too expensive for practical purposes.

After this, innumerable experiments were made on iron and copper wire ropes insulated in various ways and protected by spiral or parallel guards of iron wire and rods, and it was not until after many failures that he adopted the chain cable idea.

He appears to have used generally gutta-percha covered copper wire $\frac{1}{16}$ inch in diameter, which was protected from the chemical action of the water by a coating of sheet lead put on in spirals and secured with a spiral of tape saturated with melted wax applied hot. To protect his cables from strains and other mechanical injury, he adopted two methods—

The first, for use in rivers, where there was no navigation and no danger from grapnels, he describes as follows :—

" The gutta-percha covered wire coated with sheet lead and waxed tape is surrounded transversely with rings cut out of iron wire. Parallel to the wire, outside the rings are then placed iron rods, each $\frac{3}{8}$ inch in diameter, touching each other so as to form a bundle, like the Roman Fasces. The length of these rods is rather greater than that of the river or creek to be crossed. The rods are then secured by transverse loops of iron."

In the second method for large navigable rivers, he used a chain cable, in the angles of which a gutta-percha covered copper wire was secured. He says, that he found this chain cable a sufficient protection against the anchors and grapnels of the native craft, and that the natives soon discovered that their anchors were damaged by his chain cable, and therefore avoided anchoring in the vicinity of one.

His experiments on cables were carried out on the Huldee, and across that river he laid five experimental lines before he adopted the forms of cables described in the previous paragraphs. This is how he describes his five experimental cables—

"(1) A copper wire insulated with wax and tape.

(2) An iron wire rope.

(3) A gutta-percha covered wire undefended.

(4) A gutta-percha covered wire with defensive coating like that used between Dover and Calais.

(5) And lastly a gutta-percha covered wire secured in the angles of a chain cable.

"Of these the 1st, 2nd, 3rd and 4th were cut through by the grapnels of native craft in periods varying from one to twenty days. The last mode proved successful. The chain tears away the grapnels which hook it, and the boatmen now give the line a 'wide berth'."

In 1852, the two most important cables in circuit were those across the Huldee and Hooghly rivers. The former was 4,200 feet in length and the latter was 6,200 feet.

In the same year Sir William O'Shaughnessy states "the lines now in actual use for public business are—

		Miles.
(1) Calcutta to Diamond Harbour . . .		30
(2) Bhistopore to Moyapore (meeting No. 1 half way)		11
(3) Kookroohattee to Kedgeree . . .		25
(4) Shorter sections (including the cable across the Hooghly)		16
TOTAL .		82 "

This may be taken as the first system of telegraphs in India, for later on in the same report he says that the offices were opened for actual business on the 4th October 1851.

"Since that day four offices have been regularly in correspondence, namely, Calcutta, Moyapore and Diamond Harbour, with a reserve station at Bhistopore "

In the February following two more offices, Kedgeree and Kookroohattee, appear to have been opened on the Kedgeree line

It is curious to note that the receipts for private messages during the first three months that the telegraph was opened to the public amounted to Rs. 1,915, and that the cost of Government messages during the same period was Rs. 1,227, while the salaries of the signallers amounted to Rs. 2,530. The instrument adopted by Sir W. O'Shaughnessy for receiving signals, as before stated, was a small horizontal galvanometer locally made. The cost of the lines exclusive of the river crossings was Rs. 36,201, or about Rs. 452 per mile. Such was Sir W. O'Shaughnessy's telegraph in India in the first few months of its existence.

It was not, however, until the 1st February 1855 that the telegraph in India became an Imperial system and thrown open for the use of the general public, that previously described being simply a local system between Calcutta and places on and near the mouth of the River Hooghly.

The business done during the first complete year of working was represented by—

51,533 Private messages,
9,008 Service   „

making a total of 60,541 in number and valued at Rs. 3,10,390.

From the published reports by Sir W. O'Shaughnessy it is gathered that the lines of telegraph constructed in India

between 1st November 1853 and January 1856 extended
from Saugor Island Light House at the mouth of the
Hooghly to Peshawar, from Agra to Bombay, and from
Bombay to Madras, Mysore and Ootacamund, and there
were about two hundred and eighteen miles of line in
Pegu.

As regards the efficiency of the working he says—

"I can establish by facts and official records beyond dispute that
the Indian lines have already accomplished performances of rapidity
in the transmission of intelligence which equal that achieved on the
American lines. We have repeatedly sent the first bulletin of over-
land news in forty minutes from Bombay to Calcutta, 1,600 miles. We
have delivered despatches from Calcutta to the Governor-General of
India at Ootacamund during the rainy season in three hours, the distance being two-hundred miles greater than from London to Sebasto-
pol."

"We have never failed for a whole year in delivering the mail
news from England *via* Bombay within twelve hours, while I have posi-
tive information that Indian news sent the same distance from Trieste to
London has often during the same year been double that time in transit."

Sir W. O'Shaughnessy was absent from India, on duty
in Europe, from March 1856 to December 1857, and during
the latter year the fatal events of the mutiny occurred,
during which the destruction of a great extent of lines and
offices took place. He says in his report for 1857-58 that,
previous to his departure and up to the breaking out of the
mutiny, the lines and offices worked well and that business
was in a prosperous and advancing state, and nothing seemed
wanting to perfect the efficiency of the department but the in-
troduction of the Morse system. Then came the destruction
of the lines by the mutineers, and in the thrilling episodes
of that stormy time there is perhaps nothing more thrilling
than the story of Charles Todd, the assistant in charge of
the Delhi Office, who fell in the general massacre, but not
before he had signalled to the Punjab the terrible events
at Meerut and the march of the mutineers on Delhi. The

value of that past service of the Delhi Office is best described in the words of the Judicial Commissioner, Mr. Mont-
gomery :—*The electric telegraph has saved India.*

He continues in the same report—

" The message led to the prompt disarming of the native regiments
in Lahore and Peshawar, and as the line from Delhi to the Punjab
was, through the gallant and indefatigable services of Mr. Inspector
Brown, kept open during the whole time of the siege of Delhi, the line
and intermediate offices rendered inestimable service to the Government of India and to the highest interests of the whole Empire."

He concludes this report in the following words—

" It is now (31st October 1858) just twenty years since I erected in
the vicinity of Calcutta the first long line of telegraph ever constructed
in the world. The subject has been my occupation or pastime ever
since, and circumstances have enabled me to extend that line from
20 to over 10,000 miles. I should be destitute of all common feeling
of ambition if I did not desire most earnestly so to arrange the whole
of this vast system, that it may attain the full efficiency a short time
will accomplish, and that I may be thus enabled to make over the
Department to other management without reasonable apprehension
that the labors of my life may risk depreciation by my successors. I
trust also to witness, before I quit the field, the establishment of telegraphic communication between India and Europe, by either or both
of the proposed submarine lines. The *probability* of this communication being opened imposes upon the whole telegraph establishment
in India the urgent duty of bringing all lines and offices into the best
possible working order in preparation for that great event."

In 1857 Sir W. O'Shaughnessy introduced the Morse
system of signalling into India with great success, and in September 1858 a cable twenty-five miles in length (considered
a very long cable in those days) was laid across the Gulf of
Manaar connecting India with Ceylon with no better appli-
ances than an ordinary country sailing boat manned by a
native crew. It is also worthy of note that during this year
Sir W. O'Shaughnessy devised and brought into use the
simple expedient for protecting instruments from lightning
by the insertion of coil of fine wire in the circuit.

In his last report to Government for the year 1859-1860 he says—

" In all there are now 10,994 miles of line and 136 offices open for public correspondence   *   *. We have frequently worked direct from Calcutta to Bombay *viá* Benares, Agra and Indore, distance by the line 1,600 miles; also from Karachi to Bangalore, distance 1,800 miles   *   *   *. In January 1858 we had not more than 2,500 miles of line and 50 offices in efficient operation   *   *   *   *."

This was due to the destruction of the lines during the mutiny, for on the 1st April 1855 the system comprised 3,941 miles of line and 55 offices.

Later on he says—

" We have now 11,000 miles of lines and 150 offices (including more open in the monsoon only) and working well—a task accomplished in two years and four months "

The establishment he thus analyses—

· Superintendent in India and Ceylon. . . .	1
Deputy Superintendents, East, West and South Divisions	3
Deputy Superintendents of Circles, Rs. 400 to 500 .	10
Assistant Deputy Superintendents, Rs. 300 to 350 .	5
1st class Inspectors, Rs. 250	17
2nd „ „ „ 150 to 200	32
3rd „ „ „ 100	36
Assistant Auditor of Accounts	1
Assistant, in charge of offices, not Inspectors . .	117
Head Signallers	22
Signallers	369
Probationers	102
Sub-Inspectors	2
Overseers	5
Artificers	85
Assistant Artificers	35
Accountants, clerks, and writers	161
Mounted line guards	61
Native Artificers, Tindals, and Lascars . . .	37
Native Overseers (Jemadars)	9
„ „ (Maistries)	21

Message Examiners 11
Printers and Compositors 13
Superior workmen 6

besides line and cable guards, messengers, and office servants of all kinds.

The total cost of the establishment for all persons drawing more than Rs. 10 per mensem, he says, amounted to Rs. 68,810 in 1860 ; but with house-rent, the Bangalore workshop, line and cable guards and peons included, the salaries and wages aggregated Rs. 88,121.

The total actual expenditure in 1859-60 was Rs. 17,20,427.

The value of private messages in 1859-60 was Rs. 4,23,991.

The total number of messages sent in all India, Pegu and Ceylon in 1859-60 was—private 1,70,566, service 31,862.

He concludes the report in the following words :—

"There is a great future before the telegraph in India. By perseverance and determination it should be made the best in the world, inasmuch as it possesses a unity of organization unattainable elsewhere, with all the resources of the Empire to promote its extension and improvement. In two or at most three years from this time, the lines should yield a clear profit, and a *uniform minimum charge for messages may then be adopted for all India.* This, with the general use of some simple cypher by habitual correspondents, will enable the telegraph to perform much of the present business of the post office ; meanwhile, we have at our disposal, at a moderate cost, an instrument of such miraculous power, that by a single message it has already saved our Indian Empire, while day by day and hour by hour it is busy in the promotion of commerce and the furtherance of private interests of every kind. In my extended tours over all parts of India, I have seldom met a family who had not some anecdote to tell of the services the telegraph had done them. There are few Europeans in India who have not experienced a thrill of pleasure when they meet our masts and wires on the margin of every road, and know that these true tokens of science and civilization and power traverse our

C

Indian Empire to its uttermost limits. Should I see them no more, I can truly say that I shall ever continue to take the most heart-felt interest in the prosperity and improvement of the department and feel proud and happy that it has been my lot to bring it even to its present imperfect state."

Such is the history in brief of the telegraph in India as devised and established by Sir William O'Shaughnessy.

On the 13th June 1860 he left India on account of ill-health for England. But he was destined never to return again to the country which owes him so much. He died at Southsea at the advanced age of 80, and 29 years after leaving India.

To his indomitable perseverance and energy is due the successful establishment of the telegraph in India. The difficulties he had to overcome were of no ordinary character and had to be met with pluck, resource and ingenuity. The principle which guided him in difficult undertakings he describes himself when giving an account of the construction of the Moyapore line. He says—

" Much of this line was constructed during the rains, the welding of the iron rods having been done in canoes. The country is, in fact, a lake from June to December. I purposely selected this troublesome and objectionable line on the principle by which I have through all this undertaking been guided, that of encountering the greatest difficulties at first, so as to know the worst at once."

Such a nature was certain to succeed.

In concluding this notice of Sir W. O'Shaughnessy, it should not be forgotten that he was the first in any part of the world to construct and work a long line of telegraph.

APPENDIX.

Extracts from Notes of Lectures on Natural Philosophy

"On Galvanic Electricity"

AND

"On the Charcoal Light,"

BY

W. B. O'Shaughnessy.

CALCUTTA,

1841.

LECTURE SEVENTH.

The Galvanic Telegraph.

In this lecture I propose to give a concise account of the principle and mode of working of the various electrical telegraphs which have been contrived up to this period. The subject is one of great practical interest, and in its working details perfectly simple.

With this account I shall also embody a statement of results obtained by myself in a series of comparative experiments on a line of wire twenty-one miles in length, which I laid down for the purpose in the Botanical Gardens of Calcutta in May 1839. Of these experiments an account was published in the Journal of the Asiatic Society for February 1839.

The first electrical telegraph on record was proposed by Winkler of Leipzig in 1746. He used a Leyden jar which he discharged through a single wire and gave signals by the number of shocks passed from end to end of the line. A similar experiment was made by Le Monnier in Paris with a wire 12,789 feet long, and in 1789 Betancourt laid a wire between Madrid and Aranjuez, twenty-six miles distance, for establishing this mode of communication. Shocks, the divergence of pith balls, and sparks from pieces of tin foil were either used or proposed by various experimentalists as the direct signals to be given.

To all systems of communication by *common* electricity there is this fatal objection, that the wire employed must be perfectly insulated from the slightest contact even of damp air.

In 1807 the celebrated anatomist Soemmering proposed the employment of a galvanic battery provided with thirty-five conductors of indefinite length, each terminating in a gold pin and set in a tube containing water. His object was to decompose the water and let the extrication of gas in each tube correspond to a certain signal. This system, however, is rendered impracticable by the fact that lengthening the conducting wires beyond very inconsiderable limits annihilates the chemical force of the poles. The compound which of all others is most easily decomposed is the ioduret of potassium, and this in my experiments was unaffected at the trivial distance of three miles from a strong battery.

The deflection of the magnetic needle is the next method resorted to. In Wheatstone and Cooke's telegraph, now in operation between London and Drayton on the Birmingham road, five dipping needles are employed, which require six wires to work them, and which by combined movements of two or more needles give every variety of signal which can be required. The wires are covered with an insulating material, and are all placed for security in an iron tube led above the ground from station to station. The cost of each wire is £7 per mile; but, including the iron tube, the cost is from £250 to £300 for that distance. The needles are affected with scarcely any perceptible interval of time from making the battery contact at one extremity of the line.

Nothing can be more perfect in its action than this telegraph. The multiplicity of wires is the chief objection to its use. As I shall afterwards point out, two wires at most will suffice for a perfect system of communication, and wherever a railway or canal exists, one wire is amply sufficient. Notwithstanding the excessive delicacy of the galvanometrical needle, it is far inferior still as to the distance for which it acts, to the effects which the secondary coil machine can occasion.

Another description of galvanic telegraph was proposed by Henry of New York in 1838.

This method has attracted great attention, and is said, on good authority, to be in course of practical application in the United States.

Professor Henry proposes to employ the sudden development of magnetism, occasioned in a horse shoe bar of soft iron while surrounded by a spiral of insulated wire, the extremities of which are in contact with a voltaic couple. The magnet thus created attracts a light piece of iron which carries an arm. The arm when attracted marks dots on a revolving cylinder, or may strike a bell. A spiral wire below the centre acts as a spring to lift up the arm on the cessation of each stroke.

Eleven miles of wire were employed in one of Henry's experiments, but the wire was coiled *spirally* round a drum—a circumstance which considerably invalidates the results. This will seem sufficiently intelligible by reference to the construction of the " coil electro-magnetic machine " described in a previous page.

I now proceed to notice the results of the experiments I instituted on the comparative delicacy and efficiency of these and other systems.

My first object was to construct a line of wires of sufficient length to afford practically valuable results. With Dr. Wallich's liberal aid, a parallelogram of ground, 450 feet long by 240 in breadth, was planted with forty-two lines of bamboos. Each line was formed of three bamboos firmly driven into the ground, fifteen feet in height. Each row was disposed so as to receive half a mile of wire in one continuous line, see fig. r.

The strands of wire were one foot apart from each other. As each row was laid down, it was carefully coated with tar varnish.

A tent was pitched in front of the entire line, and the connections of the wire were so established that in the course of half an hour it could be tested from centre to the extreme flanks, so as to ascertain the effects of lengths of wire, varying from one to eleven miles at either side, forming a total circuit of twenty-two miles.

The wires employed were of iron (annealed), diameter one-twelfth of an inch. It is almost needless to observe that iron was used not from choice but necessity. The expense of copper wire would have amounted to a much larger sum than I could afford to sacrifice.

With iron wire, however, I considered that the results would be still of much practical value. Being the *worst* of the metallic conductors of electricity, it seemed a reasonable inference that whatever might be found practical with iron would *à fortiori* be so with the copper, or best conductor.

On the completion of the line the following instruments were tried :

1*st*.—An electro-magnet of soft iron, $1\frac{1}{2}$ inch in diameter, poles $\imath$ inch apart, length from centre to poles r2 inches, weight 14 lbs., surrounded by one hundred yards of insulated copper wire, the twelfth of an inch in diameter. This electro-magnet, when excited by the voltaic battery used in the subsequent experiments, with conductors, seven feet in length, supported 240 lbs.

2nd.—An electro-magnet of very small size, constructed by Watkins, of London, capable of supporting 30 lbs. with the battery now referred to, and with the same length of conductors.

3rd.—An astatic galvanometer by Watkins and Hill, already referred to.

4th.—An electro-magnetic induction or secondary coil machine.

Experiments with the electro-magnet, No. 1.

The day being fine, the ground and bamboos perfectly dry, at 9 A.M. the sustaining power of the electro-magnet, No. 1, was tested with iron conducting wires ten feet long, and found to amount to 46 lbs.

With one mile of same wire, half mile at each side—

it supported	. 18	lbs.
2 miles of wire	. 8	„ with difficulty.
3 „ of wire	. 2½	„
4 „ of wire	. 23	ounces, with difficulty.
4½ miles		. Sustaining force ceased altogether.

Electro-magnet, No. 2.

With 10 feet wire	. 12	lbs.
1 mile	. 7	„
2 miles	. 3	„
3 „	. 0½	lb.
4 „	. No sustaining power.	

Assuming iron to be inferior to copper in about the proportion of 1 to 7, according to Sir Humphry Davy's and Becquerel's standard of conductors, this experiment shews that, for equal diameters of wire, copper would convey the signal by Henry's method to about twenty-one miles in an imperceptible period of time. This distance might be extended by enlarging the diameter of the wires, but to what limit is as yet unknown.

Experiments with Galvanometer.

The astatic galvanometer was arranged and levelled with much care, the needles retaining a very slight degree of directive force so as to cause them to swing in the magnetic meridian.

At 1 mile, deviation maximum, or 90°, the needles being restrained by pins at the quadrant.

At 2 miles	.	90°
„ 3 „	.	75°
„ 4 „	.	63°
„ 6 „	.	40°
„ 10 „	.	11°
11½ miles at each side equal to total circuit 23 miles	.	Barely perceptible.

Up to the sixth mile the needles were deflected with great rapidity on the connexion being made with the voltaic element. The reversal of the order of connexion also satisfactorily reversed the needle from east to west, and the contrary. But when the deflection fell to below 40°, the movements were exceedingly sluggish, so that on an average two seconds elapsed before each signal could be read off. The change of battery poles then often failed in reversing the direction of the needles; and here, as before, at least two seconds were consumed in each movement. Applying the same rule in this as to the preceding experiment, the galvanometer would convey signals by a similar copper wire to a distance of forty-two miles; and this might be increased by enlarging the wire of the battery, or by adding to the delicacy of the galvanometer.

Induction Machine, and Mode of Correspondence by Pulsations and Chronometers.

The battery was connected with the primary coil (see fig. 2) by very short wires; and the ends of the secondary coil wires (fig. 3) screwed to the right and left wires of the great parallelogram.

On breaking contact with the primary coil, a shock utterly intolerable, passed at half a mile, to an individual holding the

D

metallic handles in which the wires ended. By this secondary coil, excited by but three small voltaic couples, the shocks up to seven miles were exceedingly smart; at eleven and a half at each side, they amounted to no more than strong, but not disagreeable sensations. I think these might be best termed "pulsations," for to the *hand* they impart the same feeling proportionately, that a strong and full pulse does to the *finger*.

Of the pulsations thus transmitted, it is perfectly easy to count six in one second; thus with a little practice any signal number can be made from one to six in one second.

Thus with copper conductors equal in diameter to the iron wires I employed, signals by pulsation are proved to be communicable by the method above described, in less than any appreciable period of time, to the distance of one hundred and fifty-four miles.

The system of correspondence which I conceive to be the simplest and most effectual is to place at each extremity of the line of two wires an induction machine and a chronometer. The dial of the chronometer is moveable and laid off with three concentric circles, each divided into twenty sections numbered and lettered as partially shewn in fig. 4. The second hand only of the chronometer is employed. If these instruments be accurate enough to keep time together for one hour, the moveable dial allows of a perfect adjustment being made, so that the second hands are invariably pointing to the same letter or number at the same time, and thus the attention of the observer has only to be aroused at the proper moment in order to give the desired signal.

This system of correspondence can be learned in half an hour. The observer has but to make himself familiar with two classes of sensations in the hands, as distinct from each other as the roll and tap of a drum are to the ear.

The *roll* is given to a person holding the handles attached to the secondary coil by rapidly turning the ratchet wheel of the first coil.

The *tap* is given by breaking contact suddenly, which is effected by pressing a metal spring (exactly like a flute key) placed in the primary circuit.

Two persons are stationed at each terminus, one say at Calcutta, the second at Agra ; one passes the signal, or records it when given to him ; the second grasps the handles, observing the chronometer dial, and at the same time he announces the signal to the other.

The annexed memorandum of instruction will explain the rest.

KEY TO THE ELECTRIC TELEGRAPH.

Attention.—A roll lasting one minute from A and returned by B.

Adjust chronometer.—(This is done by B only ; A's chronometer remains untouched.)

1. B sees when the second hand passes 60, or zero, on the dial plate, and he then gives one beat, or tap.

2. Should this beat be in advance of A's 60 mark, A gives the number of seconds so in advance in quick time and B adjusts accordingly.

3. Should the beat be behind A's 60 mark, A gives the number of seconds so behind in slow time and B adjusts accordingly.

4. When both zeros correspond, A passes three rapid rolls to signify *All's ready.*

Correspondence.

After adjustment of dials the correspondence is by numbering unless signalled to the contrary. The spelling signal is given by several rapid rolls made in quick succession.

Both in spelling and numbering.
$\begin{cases} 1 \text{ beat indicates, circle next the hand.} \\ 2 \quad \text{,,} \quad \text{,,} \quad \text{middle circle.} \\ 3 \quad \text{,,} \quad \text{,,} \quad \text{outer circle.} \end{cases}$

It may startle belief, but it is nevertheless strictly true and proved to be so by experiment, that the progress of the electric influence through a copper wire in these signals is swifter for equal distances than that of the sun's light through space. In one second it travels 244,000 miles.

Water conducts these signals with diminished rapidity, but still so rapidly that in less than a second of time the influence would pass through a longer line than the circumference of this globe.

A single insulated wire suffices for this method of correspondence, where a river or canal is available, as the second conductor.
In one of my experiments at the Calcutta gardens the electro-magnetic machine was stationed at the ghât of Bishop's College, and
one of its wires, but twenty-five feet long, dipped in the Hooghly at
the ghât.   The second wire ran along the dry pathway through the
Botanic Gardens, and terminated in Dr. Wallich's library.   A wire
led from the river at the ghât before Dr. Wallich's house, also into
the library.

The assistant stationed at the machine was directed to make
the signals in the usual manner; every signal told in the library
without any notable diminution of effect.

It made no perceptible difference whether the tide was ebbing
or flowing; in several trials even the damp mud conveyed the
signal unaltered in force or character.

The distance by water in the above experiment was 7,000 feet.
In a second set of trials the machine was placed at Sir John Royd's
garden, the water distance intervening being 9,700 feet, and with
the same results as before.

In a third trial, seven miles of wire were disposed round the
trees of the garden, taking in its entire boundary, starting from Dr.
Wallich's house and terminating in the river at Howrah; a second
wire was carried from the river, at the west end of the garden (two
miles of the Hooghly being interposed) and proceeded to the north
extremity of a canal 3,000 feet in length ; from the south end of the
canal a wire returned to the library.   Thus we had altogether
eleven miles of metallic and 13,256 feet of water circuit; the latter
in two interruptions.   The signals still passed as intelligibly and
strongly as before.

I have already stated that the cost of wire is about seventy
rupees per mile.   Under all circumstances one wire must be
insulated, and of course according to the nature of the line along
which the telegraph is laid various precautions would be requisite
to ensure its safety.   Burying the wire in a trench rammed with
pounded brick and mortar would doubtless give both insulation
and security to the extent required.   A copper wire would last for

many centuries even if exposed to the bare earth as has been sufficiently proved by the condition of the copper plates (tamba-patrás) disinterred from various localities in India. At every ten miles the wire should rise through the ground in a masonry pillar to allow of the detection of the situation of accident from earth-quakes or similar casualties.

Wherever a rail road exists the rails can be used as one conductor, and the second wire may be buried in the road without insulation. Thus, in laying out a railway of the common kind it will cost but £7 a mile, extra, to make the railway the most perfect telegraph ever yet devised. It will give signals by night or day, under every circumstance of weather, from the clerk in his closet to another at his desk, and in every conceivable variety of correspondence systems, more swift than the velocity of solar light. Electricity thus annihilates space as an impediment to the communication of ideas, and leaves the time of perception of the signal as the only source of delay.

It has often occurred to me that in India we might, for the conveyance of mails and despatches, construct at a very trivial cost a single rail along which we could transmit our dâks at treble their present speed, while as an electric telegraph the rail would at the same time transmit its lightning-like announcements of what it was bearing us along.

A single rail of hollow iron tube, one and a half inches in diameter, supported on wooden posts, would carry a light car for mails or parcels which one man could work at the rate of ten to fifteen miles the hour. Or instead of a tube, common flat bar iron might be laid down on posts with the telegraph wire securely insulated and buried in the wooden sleepers beneath. A mile of suitable bar iron would cost 176 rupees. The supports, welding, &c., would vary in cost in different parts of the line, but the wood is procurable in most places for the labour of felling.

Two coolies could work a palanquin car on a single rail at a speed of at least ten miles the hour. The expenditure of £60,000 on such a line along the Bombay road would place us in instantaneous communication with that Presidency, reduce the time of transit for our heavy mails to one-third of its present length, and provide for the conveyance of travellers at the rate of eight miles an hour at least. This plan of single rails was first proposed by Mr. Palmer, and has been adopted successfully in many parts of England and America, where, for local reasons, or the trivial returns to be anticipated, the vast outlay for the regular double rail-road could not be undertaken.

LECTURE EIGHTH.

The Charcoal Light and its Application to the Microscope, Light-houses, &c.

I have noticed, in preceding lectures, that when a powerful battery current is directed through pieces of well burned charcoal, these ignite and shed a light of such brilliancy that it transcends every other mode of illumination.

The light produced by igniting lime in an inflamed current of oxygen and hydrogen gases, though so powerful that though not larger than a pea, it casts a shadow at sixty miles distance, is inferior in illuminating effect in the proportion of two or three, to the same size of charcoal rendered incandescent by the galvanic battery. By approximative experiments it is rendered quite certain that the light from a pair of charcoal points under the influence of a powerful battery is superior to that of 500 wax lights of the ordinary size.

The charcoal must be of the firmest and densest wood : box, beech and ebony are superior to all others. It should be prepared by ignition in a covered iron crucible filled with charcoal powder and cooled without the contact of the air. With all these precautions it is nevertheless constantly found that several pieces of each lot are not susceptible of galvanic ignition. Such pieces are generally known by the dull sound emitted on their being thrown on a table. If the sound be ringing and metallic they always answer. In selecting pieces, knots should be avoided, as these are often exploded with considerable violence and danger to the apparatus employed, on the galvanic circuit being completed.

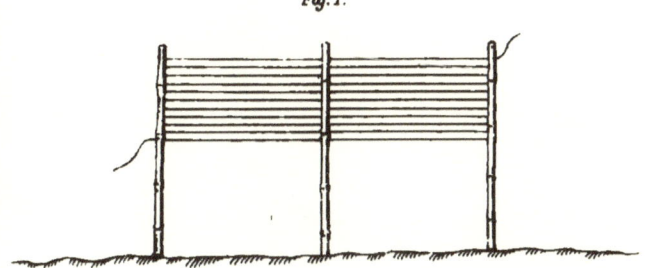

Fig. 1.

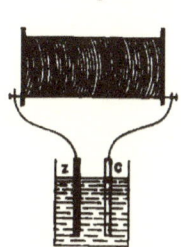

Fig. 2.

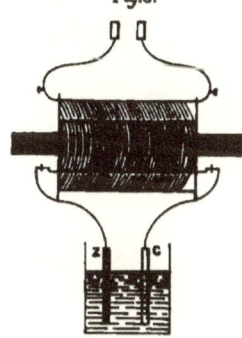

Fig. 3.

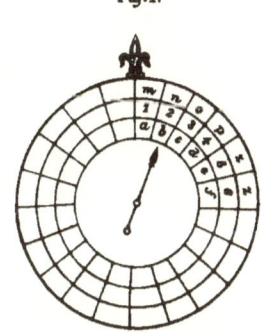

Fig. 4.

Reg. No 2611, Tel—8-9-89.—300. 100.   Litho., S. I. O., Calcutta.

The following is a simple arrangement for exhibiting this light. Two tall brass stands are provided with horizontal moveable brass arms, each terminating in a pair of copper clasps. The charcoals, one or two inches long and ¾ inch square, are inserted in these clasps and the stands are made the terminations of an extensive galvanic series. * * * * * * With the gold battery of forty-eight couples, the splendour of the light was so intense that it completely overpowered the full suit of chandeliers and wall lights in the marble hall at Government House. Their lights seemed extinguished,—their very flames were seen in deep shadow on the walls. The eye could no more endure gazing steadily on the light itself than it could on the sun at mid-day.

The chief difficulties in the practical application of this light depended on the inconstancy of the batteries formerly employed; *secondly*, on the rapid combustion of the charcoal by the air; and *thirdly*, on the expense of the galvanic power.

The first of these evils has been thoroughly overcome by the improvements recently made in galvanic apparatus. By batteries constructed on Mullin's, Grove's or my own methods, a constant and uniform supply of electricity is at our command.

To obviate the rapid combustion of the charcoal, several methods present themselves. The following has, I may say, fully answered my expectations and given us a simple mode of renewing the supply of charcoal as fast as it is required. Two copper discs three inches in diameter (each formed of two pieces of thick sheet copper kept half an inch apart and the circumference cut in radii, or so as to form a series of clasps arranged in a circle) are armed with charcoal points all round the circumference. These discs revolve horizontally and at an extremely slow rate, on spindles moved through bevel wheels by clock work. As the discs revolve, fresh surfaces of charcoal are continually presented, and by enclosing the apparatus in a common lantern a steady light can be kept up for an hour or longer. By suitable sliders and binding screws, the axle of the bevel wheels can be lengthened at pleasure so as to increase the distance between the charcoals according to the strength of the battery used.

Sir Humphrey Davy many years ago shewed that this ignition of charcoal took place *in vacuó*, the air being altogether removed, and that the arch of flame previously described was much longer in this experiment than when the air was admitted. He did not, however, pursue the subject any further, his attention being at the time directed to his celebrated and successful attempts at decomposing the alkalis and earths. Professor Silliman of Yale College in America repeated the experiment, and observed that, during the ignition *in vacuó*, the charcoal did not suffer combustion, but that small particles were transferred from one piece to the other, assuming a fused appearance. The chemical identity between pure charcoal and the diamond seems to have tempted the American philosopher to attend more to the possibility of artificially preparing these gems than to study the far more fruitful object—of applying the light evolved as a source of public illumination.

The following is a description of the vacuum apparatus I now use, and by which I have rendered the light perfectly steady, and so entirely manageable that I use it with ease for the exhibition of the splendid phenomena of the microscope. A common air-pump is employed. On the plate of this is placed a small stout copper socket for containing one of the charcoal pieces. A glass jar fits on the bell; on its upper aperture fits a ground brass plate provided with a stuffing box through which moves air-tight a copper rod terminating in a moveable clasp at the lower end, and in a binding screw at the other. The second charcoal is inserted in the clasp. One pole of the battery is twisted round the brass work of the pump, the second is screwed to the sliding rod. When this is adjusted so that ignition commences, then exhaust the air by the pump. At each successive stroke the brilliancy of the light increases, until when about half the air is exhausted (as seen by the height of the mercury in the barometer gauge) it shines forth with steady beaming fulness. Beyond this exhaustion the light becomes purplish and less fit for illumination.

Two pieces of charcoal have undergone ignition for a whole evening in this apparatus without any sensible loss of weight or any material alteration in their form.

*   *   *   *   *   *

A common exhausting syringe may be substituted for the pump, all that is required being, when the air is half removed, to prevent its re-admission by a proper valve.

There remains now but one difficulty to be overcome—namely, the expense of the electric force. My application of gilt porcelain at once meets the expense of construction; and that of a mixture of saltpetre and oil of vitriol answering perfectly instead of pure and strong nitric acid, reduces the support of the battery to a very inconsiderable expense, about ten rupees for eight hours, the light being equal to 500 wax lights for that period.

By using a very large and numerous series of zinc and copper cells, say 1,000 to 1,500, water alone or salt water at most would suffice for the excitement, and a constant light be obtained. The cumbrous nature of the apparatus would, however, more than counterbalance its cheapness.

As steam is only economical where more than the power of fifty men is required, so the galvanic light will be expensive and inapplicable to ordinary private purposes. But for light-houses, streets, and public edifices, I do not entertain the slightest doubt of its being before long adopted to the total supersession of the gas light in which we first exulted but one generation since.

Much still remains open for experiment towards the practical adaptation of this magnificent light. By careful study the quantity of light produced may be found to bear a certain ratio to a given oxidation of zinc, and as the chemical and deflagrating powers of the battery are best exerted in different arrangements of its cells, so may a new order be requisite here. The subject is one in the highest degree deserving investigation, especially by the authorities to whom the superintendence of our light-houses is entrusted.

I have only further to add that various tints may be given to the rays by previously saturating the charcoal with alcoholic solutions of salts of particular metals.

Muriate of strontium gives a deep crimson; muriate of copper a fine green; nitrate of zinc a whitish blue light. For communicating marine signals at night these facts are susceptible of ready and valuable application.